The American F

MW00886309

The flag of the United States, often referred to as 'Old Glory,' is rich with symbolism. The 50 stars represent the 50 states of the Union, while the 13 stripes recall the original 13 colonies that declared independence from Great Britain. It's a symbol of the country's enduring values: liberty, justice, and the pursuit of happiness.

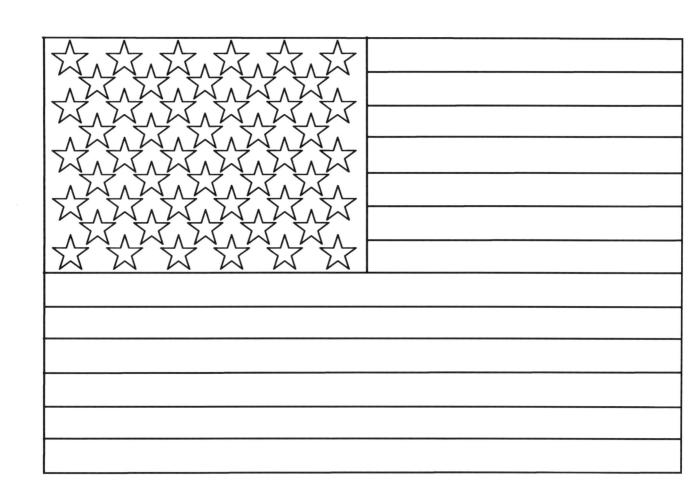

The United States of America - A Tapestry of States

From sea to shining sea, the map of the United States is a patchwork quilt of diverse states, each with its own character and story. This great nation stretches across mountains and plains, deserts and forests, with a rich history that is both shared and unique to every corner of the country. The map is not just a guide to places, but a journey through the American experience.

Independence Day

Way back in 1776, the United States gave Great Britain the ultimate "It's not me, it's you" and declared independence. Ever since, folks from all over the land come together on July 4th to celebrate their roots and what makes their country great! With fireworks lighting up the sky, friends and family gather to bask in each other's company.

The Statue of Liberty

Gifted to the United States by France in 1886, the Statue of Liberty stands as a universal symbol of freedom and democracy. Lady Liberty's torch lights the way to liberty, and her tablet inscribes the date of America's Declaration of Independence. As a welcoming sight to immigrants arriving from abroad, she represents the enduring values of a nation.

Willis Tower

Rising high above the streets of Chicago, the Willis Tower is a towering feat of architecture and engineering. Once the tallest building in the world, this skyscraper's 110 stories are a testament to the city's boldness and its sky-reaching ambitions. The Skydeck offers brave souls a chance to step out over the city, a vertigo-inducing experience with unparalleled views.

The Space Needle

Stretching 605 feet into the Seattle sky, the Space Needle is a marvel of modern engineering and a symbol of human ambition. Built for the 1962 World's Fair, this iconic tower has watched over decades of the city's growth. Its unique design was inspired by the age of space exploration, resembling a flying saucer perched atop a slender tripod. From its observation deck, visitors can gaze out at the stunning landscape, from the bustling city to the serene waters of Puget Sound.

The Empire State Building

Erected during the race to the sky in the 1930s, the Empire State Building was once the tallest building in the world, a title it held for nearly 40 years. Its 102 stories of steel and stone are a monument to human ingenuity and the dreams of a nation. From its observation decks, the city unfolds in a panorama of streets, bridges, and buildings, a living mosaic of American life.

The White House

Known worldwide as 'The People's House,' the White House serves as the official residence and workplace of the President of the United States. Steeped in American history since first erected in 1800, its hallowed halls have hosted leaders, statesmen and global dignitaries for over two centuries. As a cornerstone of American democracy, the White House standing on Pennsylvania Avenue remains one of Washington DC's most iconic sites.

The Golden Gate Bridge

Behold the majestic Golden Gate Bridge, spanning the mile-wide strait between San Francisco Bay and the mighty Pacific Ocean! This suspension bridge is a towering beauty, dressed with red-orange spires and Art Deco flair. When it was built in 1937, it was the tallest and longest suspension bridge on the planet! The bright International Orange shade was carefully chosen so it could cut through the thick fog that often blankets the bridge.

Mississippi River

The Mississippi River, known as 'Old Man River', is a lifeline of commerce and culture, flowing majestically through the United States from its source in Minnesota to the Gulf of Mexico. This river has been a highway for explorers, a border for empires, and inspiration for storytellers. Its waters nurture a diverse ecosystem and support communities along its banks.

The Grand Canyon

The Grand Canyon, a wonder of the natural world, carved by the mighty Colorado River over millions of years, stands as a testament to the earth's history. Its immense size and intricate formations are a playground for the imagination, telling stories of geology and time that stretch back to the age of dinosaurs. This colossal canyon is a mosaic of rock layers, each hue a chapter from the past.

The Sonoran Desert

The Sonoran Desert may seem quiet and still, but it's full of life and exciting secrets waiting to be discovered! This special place is the only home of the Saguaro cactus, which can grow as tall as a five-story building. Keep an eye out for the crafty roadrunner, who is much faster than it looks, and the shy Gila monster, one of the only venomous lizards in the world. Always remember, the desert is full of surprises!

Yellowstone National Park

Yellowstone National Park is a truly enchanting destination where the earth bubbles like a witch's cauldron and water shoots high into the sky. The park is home to numerous attractions, including the famous Old Faithful geyser that sprays water like a natural fountain and vibrant pools that resemble massive rainbows in the ground. It's also a vast playground for some of America's most beloved animals, such as the bison and the bear.

Yosemite National Park

Yosemite National Park is a testament to the power of preservation. Designated as a World Heritage Site for its geological wonders, the park is home to some of the tallest waterfalls, deepest valleys, and oldest and most majestic sequoias on Earth. Half Dome and El Capitan, the granite monoliths standing as sentinels over the valley, have become symbols of endurance and natural grandeur, inspiring countless visitors and artists alike.

Acadia National Park

Acadia National Park is a treasure on the coast of Maine, celebrated for its rich biodiversity and stunning landscapes. It's the oldest American national park east of the Mississippi River, featuring the tallest mountain on the U.S. Atlantic coast. Visitors can explore over 47,000 acres of trails, woodlands, lakes, and ocean shoreline, witnessing a variety of habitats that are home to a multitude of wildlife species.

Rocky Mountain National Park

Located in north-central Colorado, Rocky Mountain National Park preserves over 265,000 pristine acres of rugged mountains, flowing rivers and Aspen groves. Home to diverse wildlife like bighorn sheep and the chance to spot elk, moose and bears, the park invites exploration along 400 miles of trails with breathtaking vistas of snowcapped peaks and emerald forests. A haven for outdoor recreation and natural beauty.

Redwood Forest

The coastal redwoods of California (Sequoia sempervirens) are a testament to nature's grandeur. These ancient sentinels can live for over 2,000 years and reach heights of more than 350 feet. Their thick bark and foliage provide a unique habitat for a variety of species, and their root systems, which intertwine with those of their neighbors, create an interconnected network of support that helps them withstand the forces of nature. The redwoods play a crucial role in carbon sequestration, making them vital in the fight against climate change. These forests also hold significant cultural value for the Indigenous peoples of the region, who have lived among the redwoods for millennia. Conservation efforts continue to be critical in protecting these magnificent trees from threats such as logging and climate-related changes to their ecosystems.

The Great Lakes

The Great Lakes are a collection of five large lakes that form the largest group of freshwater lakes on Earth by total area. They hold about 84% of North America's surface fresh water and are connected to the Atlantic Ocean through the Saint Lawrence River. The lakes provide critical habitat for many species of fish and wildlife, and are a vital water source, transportation route, and recreational spot. They are named Superior, Michigan, Huron, Erie, and Ontario and are bordered by both the United States and Canada.

The Appalachian Mountains

The Appalachian Mountains are one of the oldest mountain ranges in the world, stretching for nearly 2,000 miles from the Canadian province of Newfoundland and Labrador to central Alabama in the United States. They offer a rich mix of dense forests, diverse wildlife, and a tapestry of rivers and streams. The Appalachians are known for their scenic beauty, recreational opportunities, and are home to the Appalachian Trail, a 2,200-mile-long hiking path that runs through 14 states.

Glacier National Park

Glacier National Park, located in the U.S. state of Montana, along the Canadian border, is a land of breathtaking vistas with rugged mountains, clear blue lakes, and spectacular glacial-carved valleys. The park is named for its prominent glacier-carved terrain and remnant glaciers descended from the ice ages of 10,000 years ago. It's a haven for wildlife and a treasure trove of geological history.

The American Bison

The American Bison, often called the buffalo, is the national mammal of the United States. Once on the brink of extinction due to overhunting in the 19th century, conservation efforts have helped their numbers rebound. These majestic creatures are a testament to the resilience of nature and the success of sustainable practices.

The Florida Manatee

The gentle Florida Manatee, also known as the sea cow, swims in the warm waters of the Gulf of Mexico and the Atlantic Ocean. These slow-moving herbivores are often found in shallow coastal areas and rivers where they munch on water grasses, weeds, and algae.

The California Quail

Say hello to the California quail, also known as the valley quail, which is the state bird of California. These charming birds have a unique topknot that looks like a single feather bouncing as they move. They are social birds often found in groups, or 'coveys.' The male's vivid markings and the female's more subdued colors help them blend into their surroundings, making them a delightful challenge to spot on your next outdoor adventure in California's wilds.

The Maine Lobster

The Maine Lobster, famous for its delicious taste, is a crustacean that thrives in the cold, clear waters of the North Atlantic. Lobster fishing is an important industry for the coastal communities of New England and is regulated to ensure sustainability for generations to come.

The Bald Eagle

The bald eagle, chosen as America's national bird, has a majestic appearance and historic significance as a symbol of freedom. They have a wingspan of up to 7 feet and are found across the U.S. and Alaska. They primarily feed on fish, but also hunt small mammals, birds, and carrion. Bald eagles are impressive hunters and can dive at speeds of up to 100 miles per hour. They mate for life, build large nests in trees near water sources, and are important apex predators in the ecosystem. Despite being once endangered due to habitat loss and hunting, conservation efforts have helped to increase their population.

The Gray Wolf

The gray wolf is an iconic symbol of the Western United States. Highly intelligent and social hunters, gray wolves usually live and travel in packs. Once nearly extinct across the lower 48 states due to human persecution, gray wolf populations are recovering thanks to conservation efforts. Colorado, Minnesota, Idaho and other Western states now host growing gray wolf families in forest and mountain environments.

Alaska Moose

As the largest member of the deer family, magnificent moose inhabit the diverse ecosystems of The Last Frontier. With spectacular antlers and an unmissable profile, these shy herbivores can often be spotted wading in lakes and streams or browsing through boreal forests. As the iconic animal embodying the untamed wilderness of interior Alaska, moose appear on the state flag and remain a symbol of natural splendor.

The Monarch Migration

The monarch migration is an impressive journey for millions of butterflies from the US to their wintering sites in the mountainous forests of Mexico. Their migration is crucial for their survival and involves multiple generations using environmental cues like the magnetic field and the sun's position to navigate. The monarch's dependence on milkweed and specific climatic conditions for their survival makes them a symbol of the need for ecological conservation.

The Apple Pie

In kitchens across America, the sweet aroma of baking apple pie weaves through the air, a symbol of comfort and tradition. Granny's apple pie, with its buttery crust and cinnamon-spiced filling, is a slice of happiness just waiting to be shared. Every apple, from tart Granny Smiths to sweet Golden Delicious, plays its part in creating this timeless dessert.

Barbecue

Barbecue isn't just about cooking meat; it's a whole vibe, a cultural experience that brings folks together. From east to west, every region has its twist on this mouth-watering tradition. Barbecue love is like a kaleidoscope, a colorful mix of flavors as diverse as the great country.

Deep-dish Pizza

Deep-dish pizza is a special kind of pizza that comes from the city of Chicago in the United States. Unlike other pizzas, deep-dish pizza has a high edge and a thick crust, and it's baked in a deep pan. The toppings are layered with cheese at the bottom, then meats and vegetables, and finally, the sauce on top. This delicious treat is like a pizza pie, and it's a favorite for many people around the world!

Baseball

Baseball, affectionately known as America's pastime, is a sport of strategy and skill. Two teams take turns batting and fielding, with the goal of scoring runs by hitting a ball and circling four bases to return to home plate. A game is divided into nine innings, where each team tries to outscore the other. Pitching and batting are at the heart of the game, while defensive plays like catches and throws are key to preventing runs. The blend of individual performance and team dynamics makes baseball a captivating sport that has endured for over a century.

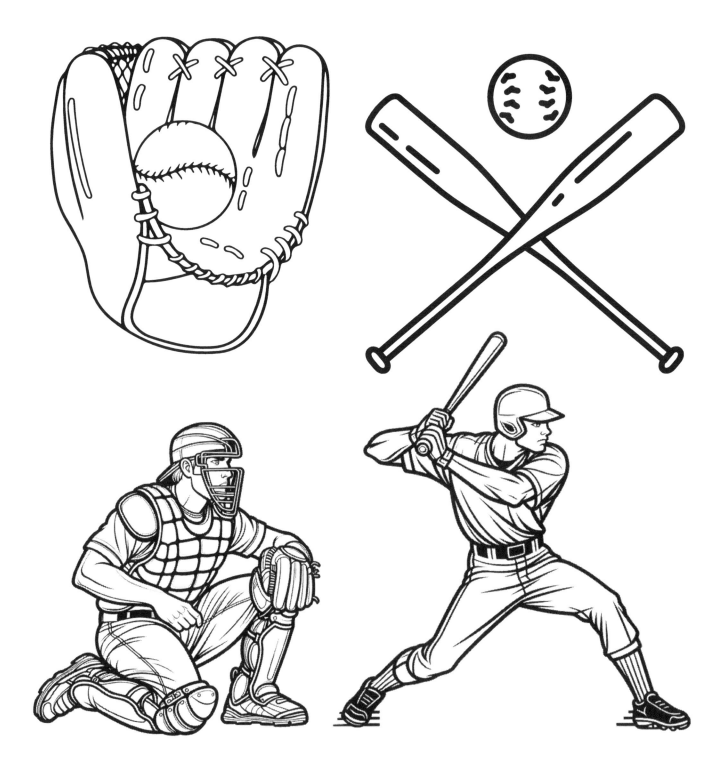

Basketball

Basketball, an iconic American invention, is a sport woven into the cultural fabric of the United States. Created in 1891 by Dr. James Naismith, it quickly became a staple in schools and professional leagues across the nation. The game pits two teams against each other on a rectangular court, vying to score points by shooting a ball through a hoop elevated ten feet above the ground. Embodying the American spirit of innovation and competition, basketball is played in four high-octane quarters that highlight the players' prowess in dribbling, passing, and shooting. With the global influence of the NBA, basketball not only serves as a testament to American ingenuity but also as an enduring symbol of its cultural impact.

American Football

American football, a sport that is quintessentially American, stands as a powerful emblem of the nation's competitive spirit and love for complex strategy. Emerging from college-level play in the late 19th century, it has evolved into a game deeply embedded in the cultural identity of the United States. Played on a 100-yard field, the sport features two teams contending to score points by carrying or passing a ball into the end zone. With its intricate playbook, distinct positions, and the celebrated Super Bowl—America's most-watched annual television event—American football captures the essence of American teamwork, resilience, and tactical ingenuity like no other sport.

Ice Hockey

American football, a sport that is quintessentially American, stands as a powerful emblem of the nation's competitive spirit and love for complex strategy. Emerging from college-level play in the late 19th century, it has evolved into a game deeply embedded in the cultural identity of the United States. Played on a 100-yard field, the sport features two teams contending to score points by carrying or passing a ball into the end zone. With its intricate playbook, distinct positions, and the celebrated Super Bowl—America's most-watched annual television event—American football captures the essence of American teamwork, resilience, and tactical ingenuity like no other sport.

NASA and Space Exploration

NASA, which stands for National Aeronautics and Space Administration, is the organization responsible for America's space missions and scientific discoveries in space. It has sent astronauts to the Moon, rovers to Mars, and telescopes into orbit to look deep into space. Space exploration helps us to learn about our universe, from the planets in our solar system to the farthest reaches of space. It's an adventure like no other, filled with mysteries waiting to be solved and wonders to be discovered.

Silicon Valley

Silicon Valley is a nickname for a part of California that is famous for being a powerhouse of technology and innovation. It's where dreamers and thinkers build the future! This is the birthplace of the world's favorite gadgets and websites. Companies like Apple, Google, and Facebook grew up here, changing the way we talk, play, and learn. It's not just about computers and code, but about bright ideas that light up the world. The people in Silicon Valley imagine what tomorrow could be and then make it happen!

America's national flower

The rose, with its stunning petals and enchanting fragrance, holds a special place in the heart of America as the nation's official floral emblem. This beloved flower symbolizes the love, honor, and devotion found in the American spirit. Across the United States, from private backyards to the celebrated Rose Garden at the White House, roses bloom in a dazzling array of colors, each one telling a story of beauty and resilience. When you gaze upon a rose, you're not just looking at a flower—you're witnessing a living piece of America's heritage and the timeless values it represents.

American Beautyberry

Deep in the heart of American woodlands and gardens, the American Beautyberry bush weaves a spell of purple magic. As summer turns to fall, this remarkable plant bursts into a spectacle of shimmering purple berries, each one like a tiny jewel. These berries aren't just a feast for the eyes; they're a banquet for wildlife, too, providing food for birds and other animals as the days grow cooler. The American Beautyberry is more than just a pretty face—it's a symbol of the wild and wondrous corners of America's great outdoors.

Sunflower

Standing tall and turning its face to follow the sun across the sky, the sunflower is like a little piece of sunshine rooted to the earth. This cheerful bloom is not only beautiful but also useful—its seeds are a tasty treat and can even be made into oil for cooking. Sunflowers symbolize loyalty, adoration, and longevity, and they are known for being happy flowers, bringing joy to all who see them. With their bright yellow petals, sunflowers capture the warm glow of summer days and the spirit of American farmlands.

The California Poppy

Imagine a field shimmering with gold – that's what a meadow of California Poppies looks like in full bloom! Known as the 'Golden Poppy,' this bright flower paints the hills and valleys of California with its radiant orange hues every spring. The California Poppy is more than just a pretty face; it's a resilient plant that can thrive in the wild, bringing a splash of color to even the driest of landscapes. When you color in these poppies, remember that each one is a symbol of the Golden State, reflecting the sunny spirit and natural beauty of California.

Tulip

Each spring, tulips bring a burst of color to gardens and parks across America, signaling the arrival of warmer days. These elegant flowers come in almost every color you can think of, from sunny yellows and fiery reds to cool purples and even striped varieties! Tulips stand for perfect love and have a special place in celebrations and festivals in several states where they are honored as a symbol of growth and renewal. Known for their simple yet striking beauty, tulips capture the joy of spring and the spirit of American traditions in gardening.

Made in the USA
Las Vegas, NV
19 February 2024

85970472R00048